The Crew

No one plays by the rules

Andrew Barrett

The Ink Foundry

Preface

Proud to swear in British English.

Contents

Readers Club Offer

See the Readers Club download offer at the end of this book.

PART ONE

Chapter One

The Favour

THIS WHOLE JOB WENT tits-up before I even got involved.

You know when something bad happens during your day and you sit down for your evening meal – a Pot Noodle and a tin of beans – looking back on it, wondering where it all went wrong, wondering if you could have spotted the signs? Wondering if you could have prevented that something bad from happening?

I knew I'd spend a lot longer than one evening looking back on today, but in my defence, there wasn't anything I could have done to give today a happy ending. Sometimes other people jump into your life; you're just one more pavement slab under their feet, just one more step on their life journey. They step on you, mess up your day, mess up your life, and you don't have any say in the matter.

Today, I was someone's step on their life journey. I didn't enjoy it much.

My shift was a late – I started at 3pm and if fate was on my side, I'd get finished at 11pm. And to make matters worse, this was day seven of a seven day stretch. Being a CSI here in Leeds is hard enough, but by the beginning of day seven you're aching and hurting, and your head doesn't belong to you anymore, and you can't even remember what it's like to be home with a cup of coffee in your hand with nothing better to do. You don't get a chance to feel bored doing this shit – the days merge, the weeks merge; even Christmas Day is just like any other but with added arseholes – people being even more pissed than usual, and there's tinsel everywhere. There are no special days – except the ones where you're not here.

But today – day seven – was about to get even worse.

"Eddie?"

That's my gaffer. He's the sort of person I don't get along with. Let's be clear about something: I don't get along with many people. Those I get along with best happen to be dead – if it wasn't for the smell, they could be my best friend on account of they don't talk back and they don't force their opinions on you or ask you for favours. Yep. Live people do all that and more. Fucking annoying. And he's no different.

"Can you do me a favour?"

See what I mean?

And then he stepped aside, waved a hand at the woman standing behind him. "This is Shannon." And then he left it hanging as though I was supposed to infer something.

I nodded at Shannon. Looked at my gaffer.

"Can you take her out?"

"I'm not looking for a relationship, right now. But thanks for the offer."

"Eddie."

I did one of those long blinks. No idea how it looked from the outside, but in here it looked amazing. "What? An attachment?"

He nodded. Shannon went red; it clearly wasn't the reaction she'd hoped for.

"Day seven. Lates. An attachment?" Just what I need – an observer riding along with me, spoiling my solitude.

"Sorry." And then he walked away.

Sorry. He didn't even try to engage in pseudo-negotiation, something like, 'Would you mind? It'll get us out of a tight spot. Double booked; I'll knock your next two attachments. Is that okay?' Nothing like that at all. Just, "Sorry".

I sighed. It's my favourite thing. A sigh can say a thousand words without me having to think of any. Anyway, I looked at her, and she was still red. It wasn't her fault; we usually take out attachments on the early shift; they add a burden to our already heavy workload, and they seem easier to deal with in daylight hours.

Yeah, I know; I can hear your violin from here. We don't have a heavy workload compared to road-workers, miners, carers… but it's heavy on the mind, and you don't need someone peering over your shoulder, trying to understand what you're doing and why, when they don't really need to. They're there to observe and to say they've been out with a CSI – it's part of the modern culture of ticky-box policing.

Sometimes coming out with a CSI on attachment is mutually beneficial. New coppers come out with us – and that's a great idea because they're often first to a crime scene and what you can show them today might stop them fucking up one of your scenes in a few months' time. Often, our attachments are here out of curiosity, and that gets old pretty quickly. Basically, you're their entertainment for the day.

They're taking one of the two seats in your van. That second seat is your desk for the mountains of paperwork you need to do for each job these days. No fun having someone sitting on your desk when you're trying to look at the images on the back of a camera and write the titles for them; no fun when you're trying to write down bag numbers for the dozens of exhibits that are sliding around all over the floor. It's embarrassing for them, and probably boring too, but it's fucking annoying for us.

On top of this, you have to mind your manners. You can't just lift a cheek and let rip any more. No, you have someone sitting on your desk, remember?

I nodded to her and we left the office, having said a cheery goodbye to my colleagues. After the door swung closed behind us, I heard a cheer go up. It made me smile.

Once in the van, I do all the pre-flight checks – because if the force can think of ways to give you extra paperwork, they won't miss the opportunity, believe me. And I'm building up to asking her a question. I don't want to, but I have no choice. I look across at her, did a quick appraisal. She was the kind of woman who walked around with a sadness in her eyes, glossing them up; like everything had turned bad inside and the smile was the casual lie of everyday window-dressing. "Where do you work?"

She cleared her throat. "I'm in personnel."

I stared at her. If I'd had a mouthful of coffee right then, she would have been wearing it.

"I'm interested in CSI, though. Would love to be one."

Yeah, of course you would, I think. "Must get boring," I said, "being in an office all day?"

"Can I be honest?"

That made me sit up. "Sure."

"I fucking hate it."

I fell in love just a little bit there and then. She spoke my kind of language – I use two of those four words approximately six-hundred-thousand times a day. 'I' and 'it' are not the ones in case you haven't worked it out yet. "Why do you do it, then?"

She shrugged. "It was a way into the force. I'd like to try for CSI when some positions come up."

I fired up the van, hit buttons left, right, and centre, to stop the bleeps and bings and bongs and flashing lights that they fit these days. I wish I could find the wires for them; I'd rip them all out – it's like driving a fucking disco.

"Bravo Seven-Two," I said into the radio mic.

"Bravo Seven-Two. Go ahead."

"Code Five. For your info I'm out with an attachment. Someone from personnel."

It took them a while to get back to me with an acknowledgement. They were busy laughing at me, that's why. Eddie Collins out with someone from personnel – must've seemed like poetic justice.

"One-Twenty."

Bitch. They were all laughing at me. I didn't care, let them laugh. I looked across at her. "Shannon, eh?"

She nodded, mouth zipped up tighter than a body bag, hands in her lap, knees together.

Wow, this was going to be an exciting evening.

But when she asked if we could nip to Mac's, grab a coffee, and maybe pull over for a cigarette, I almost had a semi on.

Chapter Two

Introspection Second

WE DID SCENE EXAMINATIONS at two burglaries and photographed an assault victim's injuries. They weren't especially interesting jobs. In fact, the most interesting one was in a high-rise tower block. Number 152. Fifteen floors up. One look out of the window had me clinging to the walls, heart banging away like a bitch, teeth gritted until my jaw ached. I hate heights. I did my best to keep my anxiety under wraps, but when we finally returned to earth and the door to the block slammed behind me, I breathed out air that was almost an hour old.

"Not keen on heights, then?"

"It showed?"

No, they weren't especially interesting jobs, but they *would* have been of interest to those police officers young in service that I already mentioned. And to her credit, Shannon paid attention, was asking all the right questions, and keeping out of the way – which I always like. I have a job to do, and though I'm trying to impart my knowledge and rationale, my priority is the victim – I do my job for them. I tell coppers, and I told her, to keep an eye for footwear marks – they're easily left, and easily damaged. I like footwear marks, and I go well out of my way to get them.

I'm not going to catch the burglar for them. Probably eighty percent of the time, I find nothing at a crime scene, nothing that's of interest to the investigating officer, anyway. But what I can give is a good public service. And I'm very keen on making sure these people get their money's worth – they're paying me to help them and help them I will. Even if it's only in reassurance, or maybe some crime prevention advice; maybe it's only to lift their spirits… hey hold up, I know what you're thinking – how the hell can Eddie Collins lift anyone's spirits?

Easy. I care about these people who someone has used as a paving stone to get what they want, or to get where they want. They are the downtrodden. They mean a lot to me and if I can help their mental state, I will. I've seen people crumble because they got burgled and it's not at all nice.

Shannon did well, she showed empathy and was respectful to the victim and to me. She came into the house of the second burglary about ten minutes after I did. I was a little unfair to her. I knocked on the door and a young woman answered. "Hi, police fingerprints," I said by way of an introduction.

"Oh hi," she said, stepping aside.

"I understand someone smashed your back door in." I kept my face dead straight and beside me, Shannon wheeled around and was off back down the garden path, shoulders hitching up and down as she tried to hide the laughter. Gets 'em every time.

* * *

After I finished the job, I pulled the van around the corner, somewhere reasonably discreet so I could write my notes up in peace and she could stand at the open van door and smoke as twilight collapsed under the onslaught of night.

It was cold. I could see streetlamps shining orange through the steam coming from people's boilers. A whole row of them – looked like a dozen smokers lined up on a permanent exhale. I could see down to the valley where a beck trickled along, and mist sat there like smoke in a bowl.

She stayed outside and closed the van door because the temperature was dropping and I was trying to type up my notes, and that's not a ten-minute job these days. The government have taken an interest in what we do and have done their level best to royally fuck it up. One of the wonderful ways they've fucked it up is to put people in charge who don't know shit about the job and pump a crapload of rules into the system that are nothing short of stupid.

I ignore those rules whenever possible. But one of the things I can't ignore – because the spineless gaffers who agree to all the bullshit coming down from above can check easily enough – is the paperwork. It takes an age, and is so long-winded that police officers, who want to read what I've done at a crime scene and what I found that might help them, can't see that because of the chapters of shite they have to wade through first. It makes me weep when I think of what they're doing to the job.

But anyway, she'd closed the door and sealed me inside. She leaned against a fence, looking into a small dark parkland. Pretty white lamps shone along a pathway that threaded from one side to the other in a meandering fashion. I leaned back in my seat, cracking my back, stretching my arms, and rubbing my tired eyes. I threw the Bluetooth keyboard on the passenger seat and stepped out, knees popping.

I propped myself against the fence a yard or two from her and lit up my own smoke. She was looking away from me. "Still want to do this job?" I asked.

She sniffled, nodded.

I'm known throughout Leeds for my people skills and my ability to engage in small talk. I have a certificate and everything. "Suppose anything's better than working in personnel." I flicked ash. "Except intelligence. Gotta be dumb to work in intelligence." No response from her. Yes, I know, I'm not here to entertain her, and I'm certainly not here to lift her mood. What the hell do I care if she's crying while she's staring away into the distance. I don't, right? "Come on," I said, "let's get back in the van. It's so cold out here my dick looks like a Walnut Whip."

Once back inside, the interior light showed me that she *had* been crying. It could have been my scintillating company – it's happened before, but I doubted it. Shannon came to the game with pre-engaged sadness, and all it took was something trivial to open up the taps. "What?" I asked. I didn't really want to expand on that; just what would do for now.

"I'm okay. Feel a bit melancholy." She finished with a shrug and looked at me as though this was my cue to step in and cheer her up.

That put me in a bit of a spot. I'm not good at that kind of thing; it's not my forte. I licked my lips. "You want me to drop you back at the nick? You can piss off home and cry into a glass of Chardonnay." She was already shaking her head. "What then?" I asked. "You can't come into the next burglary scene like this unless you've got The Samaritans phone number with you."

She tried to laugh, but by any standards it was a fucking poor effort. "I don't want to go home. It's empty there," she said.

I was confused. "That's a bad thing, right? Only, it's my perfect evening."

"Me and..." She looked at me.

I waited. Why can't people finish their sentences? Huh? I'm not a fucking clairvoyant. I'm useless at guessing games. I waited some more, sighed. Tapped my fingers on the steering wheel. "You're going to have to give me a bigger clue."

"It's complicated," she said.

"Right," I said. "Are you okay to carry on? There'll be more jobs coming our way." She deflated a bit, and I got the impression I missed my calling as a social butterfly: I definitely should have asked her something more meaningful, something about her feelings or about— wait, I got it! "Is this about a relationship?"

She nodded and pulled out a hanky.

Christ, I was on fire! "You up for the next job, then?"

She dabbed her eyes, then looked at me hurt, as though I had no compassion.

The triumphant smile left my face. "What?"

"You have no compassion."

I was right again. I was getting good at this!

"Bravo Seven-Two."

Trying not to look as though I was thanking God for the interruption, I hit the button and said, "Go ahead."

"Are you Code two? We have a P1 in Meanwood. Armed robbery." Enthused, I said, "Hit me."

"If only I could," Control said. I didn't know they had a sense of humour in there. I thought one of the stipulations of their job was having no sense of humour. "It's at a Post Office." She passed the rest of the details, and I buckled up, looked across at Shannon.

"You'll enjoy this one," I said. "Take your mind off... cheer you up." In the light from the overhead lamp I could see damp tracks down her cheek. I wanted to offer her a tissue, but I didn't have any, and then I wanted to get her out of my van. I don't like emotions – especially in other people, and double especially when I was expected to deal with it or offer her support. I'm not a welfare officer, I'm a CSI, and my emotional support extends to those people who are victims of crime, not those who are just a poor judge of lover.

Was I being too harsh? I expect I was; she was a nice lass and she was obviously going through something upsetting. And no matter how often you're told to keep your home life at home, it's inevitable some of it will stow away, ready to jump ship when you least expect it, or when you're least prepared for it. Just like you're told not to take your work home with you, I suppose. I'd like to say that I never took my work home, that I can switch off as soon as I close the office door… but that wouldn't be telling the truth. I've dragged all kinds of ghosts through my house when they should have stayed in the office, and sometimes they stay for weeks at a time.

Sometimes they move in permanently.

I looked at the tablet, searching for that Post Office job, but my mind was wondering how to help Shannon, and it was also wondering how I could become more compassionate. I was a failure where my fellow humans were concerned, and it began to bother me. Maybe we all needed a hug every now and then.

She sniffled again and I found the Post Office job, scanned the log, and noted the estimated value: seventy-five grand. Wow, what the hell were they doing with that kind of money within reach? There was no mention of forcing the postmaster to open safes or anything like that. This was going to be an interesting job; thoughts of helping humankind fled, as did thoughts of helping Shannon. I know, I'm a selfish twat – job first, introspection second.

Chapter Three

The Gardener

WE ROLLED UP TO the cordon as the rain arrived. It's almost predictable, isn't it, English weather? If there's something important to do, you can guarantee it'll fucking rain. Now I'm not saying there was anything important outside to examine anyway, but chances are there would be an escape route to check at the very least, and who needed rain when you were trying to check for footwear marks or blood or whatever, with litter blowing through it, taking the piss.

The only good thing about the rain was that it masked Shannon's still-damp cheeks. No one would ever know she was a blubbing wreck only fifteen minutes ago – and that included me; I could conveniently forget all about it and get to work without worrying if she needed a new Kleenex.

Yes, I know.

I turned off the engine and peered through the screen at the scene tape fluttering in the wind, at the uniformed coppers standing at the front door of the Post Office trying to keep warm, at a huddle of CID officers beneath an awning, that created its own waterfall, waiting for me. I looked across at Shannon. "If you want, stay in the van and have a smoke – just crack the window though, eh."

She shook her head. "I'd like to come with you."

Great.

"If you don't mind."

Well fucking cheer up then, miserable cow.

"I promise to cheer up a bit."

I looked at her, almost asked if she could read minds – she was so spooky. "Come on then."

It was like a gathering of the dejected. All of us in the Post Office just inside the double front doors, CID wishing we'd just get on with it, us wishing they'd just naff off so we could do our job. But we needed the briefing first. This was where we harvested everything they knew about the job and learned what they needed to prove. Everything they said usually had a handful of errors thrown in there too. But that was okay – I took everything anyone told me with a bath full of salt. No one's perfect, stories get skewed, facts get blurred; it's all part of the job.

You take an initial story, and then you ignore it, let the evidence speak up, let it confirm or deny what you've been told. And then it's your turn to enlighten CID with what you believe actually happened, and what proof you had. It's all a big game, batting shit back and forth until you meet on common ground. I like to think of this stage, the forensic scene examination stage, as the most important aspect of an investigation – people's freedom depended upon it, and other things depended upon what you found too. Whether the postmaster got to keep his job, whether the insurance company would cough up, that kind of thing.

So doing your job with one eye on the clock was absolutely no way to commence a scene examination. You forget about everything else, put to the back of your mind that CID might want answers quickly, because that's just asking for trouble – you've only got half a story, you've only found half the evidence, so you're giving them guesses, and no one should rely on guesses.

Do the job, then talk about it.

DS Tanner played liaison officer, introducing us to an Irish DI from New Scotland Yard who'd been tasked with traipsing across the country every time a robbery with this kind of MO happened. Tanner said DI Wilbourne was building a picture of the offenders, who by now had become quite famous in southern England, and had noted their journey north. You could tell that he was itching to nail them – all he needed was that one crucial piece of evidence that would give him a name. So far, Wilbourne admitted, they had nothing. "They're like ghosts," he said.

All our evidence would go through him, and he would coordinate its submission. Our force was keen on him being here, and when he said that the Met was picking up the forensic bill, I could see why.

DS Tanner then waved us goodbye – probably didn't want to miss the manager's special at KFC; he left us to the mercy of this 'foreign' DI. We had a local DC as our point of contact.

Shannon stood by my side, and we stared at Wilbourne as he delivered his assessment of the information he'd been given from eyewitnesses, possible CCTV footage, and victims… you get the idea. It pays to give it your full attention, but I couldn't.

Wilbourne was like a tramp with a suit on – and I call it a suit because I don't know what the collective term for old gardening clothes is; he just needed muddy wellies to complete the ensemble. He had a hippy's beard, and small greasy spectacles with raindrops still clinging to them. What stood out most for me, except his soothing Irish lilt, were the hairs almost an inch long sticking out of his nostrils, and my eyes found them twitching as he spoke and chose them to focus on. I missed most of what he said because inside I was laughing my bollocks off. But I began to get annoyed because they were sapping my concentration, then I got edgy, just wanting him to leave so I could begin.

A young, and I might add, quite pretty, local DC, whose surname slipped by as my mind grappled with her forename – Jennifer – stared at me as I took Wilbourne's briefing. I could feel her eyes studying me as mine studied those nasal hairs. And all at once I found myself smiling. You shouldn't really smile during a briefing, it's supposed to be serious; it's going to contribute to the basis of your scene exam, but I was smiling, nonetheless. Those hairs, Jennifer's eyes. Didn't *she* notice the hairs? Didn't *she* find them funny or distracting – maybe she'd learned to ignore them.

I found myself giggling, and I knew I'd better choose something everyone could find funny, or at least understand, before I pointed at the hairs and howled.

"Sorry," I said, "some idiot youths out there dicking about." I cleared my throat as everyone turned to see for themselves. "They've gone now." I bit the inside of my cheek as hard as I could just as the nasal hairs came back into view. I wanted to laugh. I took my mind off them by turning slightly and staring right back at Jennifer. Our eyes locked and, luckily for me, she looked away as Wilbourne resumed his monologue. She was a lot prettier than a clump of curly grey hair; I could see the heartbeat in her neck, a slender gold chain tracing the contours of her throat bobbing up and down with each beat.

I bit my other cheek, made myself focus.

Gordon Ramsay – who was no relation to the TV chef, Wilbourne stated from the off – had been cashing up behind the counter. His brother, and co-owner of the premises, was out of the store. Sixty-year-old Gordon was manning the till, and to his right was an open door into the cash office, where both safe doors were wide open.

That prompted an exchange of looks between all four of us. That look said Inside Job. So that was one theory I'd keep in mind as I carried out my examination. No one has seventy-five grand on show in a shop they're alone in, breaking every rule in the Post Office's book about safes and cash offices and about staff levels during cashing up. Of course, I didn't know their rules – but I bet they had some!

Mr Ramsay was without a paddle, it seemed.

"Two males entered. Shouting and screaming. Brandishing weapons."

"What weapons?" I asked.

"Machetes," Wilbourne said.

"And possibly a handgun," Jennifer casually slid that little one in there.

"And possibly a handgun," Wilbourne repeated.

"Mr Ramsay was unable to close the doors or the safes before two youths leapt over the counter and began beating him to the ground. This has come from the ambulance. He mumbled all of this as they were taking him to the Leeds General."

I was fine running with a part-baked story for now. It would all become clear before much longer. "CCTV?"

"No." Jennifer took a deep breath. "Only Gordon knows how to operate it, and he's in ICU."

"But it's Post Office—"

"We know. We'll have a copy first thing in the morning. But for tonight," Wilbourne shrugged, "can't help you."

Great. I don't rely on CCTV, but it can be a good guide, and it can save lots of time. No point in me examining every counter if I know from CCTV that they jumped over just one section of it. Ah well…

"We reckon it took less than two minutes," Jennifer said. "There's a petrol station opposite and someone was filling up, leaning against their car, and they saw these males enter, and then a short while later saw them exit again with Ramsay screaming after them covered in blood before he collapsed. They ran around the building—"

"There's a back street," Wilbourne cut in. "We've got it guarded."

"Two in, three out?" I asked.

They both nodded. "So far as we know," Jennifer said.

"We okay to leave it with you?"

I love hearing those words – they're my favourites. "I think I can manage," I said.

Wilbourne checked his watch. "It's six-thirty. If we come back at nine?"

"Yep," I said. "You leaving officers front and rear?"

They nodded, as they reached out for the door handle. I knew they'd keep a guard on, with there being a mention of a firearm involved, but I like to make sure no one has any silly ideas about pulling my guards away and leaving me vulnerable.

"And we have an ARV here too."

"Excellent," I said, ushering them to the door. "One more thing. Ramsay, is he going to die?"

"No, don't think so. He was still unconscious last we heard, but they're optimistic he'll pull through."

Ah, alone at last. I looked up and Shannon was there. Okay, not quite alone.

"How do you want me to play this?" she asked. "Shall I ask questions as you go along, or shall I just keep my trap shut?"

PART TWO

Chapter Four

Nelson's Job

THIS WHOLE JOB WENT tits-up before I even got involved.

We're very close, us four.

Ever seen *Full Metal Jacket*? Yeah? Well, that's us. Close, like brothers. Ain't nothing we wouldn't do for a brother. Nothing.

I'm Nelson. I'd like to think they called me Nelson after the battles he won, Trafalgar and the like. Top bloke he was. But they don't call me Nelson after him. No, they call me Nelson after that little bastard from *The Simpsons* who laughs like he just farted. I laugh like that. Can't help it. Not bothered anyway, 'kay?

So there's me, Kale – because he likes weed, and kale is like a weed, see? Then there's Zak – he's Polish and no one can pronounce his fucking name, but it's got a lot of zeds in it. We could have called him Zed, but it don't have the same ring to it, see? Who else? Ah yea, there's Dandy. We call him Dandy cos he's a gay black man who's well over six-foot tall. Seriously, that bastard could have been a pro basketball player. But he was too busy chasin' boys to be bothered with it. And we call him Dandy cos it's like the direct opposite of what he looks like, see? He likes it.

We've been together for six years and we work well. We used to do jewellery shop robberies – daylight, full on, man. In and out in five minutes before the law gets its arse in gear. Trouble with jewellery jobs these days is fencing the stuff. The return is shite, and trust is a long way down the list of priorities for these arseholes who ship it abroad. They'd rather do you over, shop you, or clip your wings and try and recruit you, or spin you out to that manor's gang. Seriously, it was getting more dangerous to cash that shit than it was to do the fucking job.

So we looked around at other things. Cash in transit was the obvious way to go, but recently, the tech behind them jobs has got beyond us. Days gone by you'd pop a guard and take the box of dosh, smash the fucker with a sledgehammer and happy days. Not now, you so much as breathe near it and the fucker explodes and covers you in red dye. Not worth it, seriously, we've tried.

We did a few bookies in London when we started out. That's usually good for a few quid, but it's risky too. Most of the customers are skinny toothless losers who wouldn't say fuck all to a couple of masked men walking by them, know what I mean? But there was the have-a-go-heroes that thought they was Schwarzenegger, and fancied getting a name for themselves, and probably fancied Beryl who worked behind the counter, and would try to impress her. Sometimes these geezers wound up dead, and Beryl ain't turned on by dead men. Still, they usually get a small golden plaque on the wall by the gents'. So that's nice.

When the adrenaline is running hot, man, and you just want to nick a feller on the arm or maybe break his nose… it sometimes goes further, and you cause serious damage. Regrettable. But funny as fuck.

Even the bookies was getting harder and harder to hit. Fucking CCTV everywhere, cash tills regularly emptied, so you end up doing a job for pennies. And nothing makes me more angry than pulling a job off and getting paid in change, know what I mean? We have expenses, equipment, food and lodgings, travel. It's not free, you know; someone has to pay, and it comes out of our profit. No one likes negative equity.

Negative equity. Yep, I watch the BBC news, I know the lingo.

We been together since just after school. Zak and me went to a builder's college and we lasted less than a year. That was some serious hard fucking work for a pittance – fucking government and their apprentice scheme bred a couple of armed bandits instead of brickies; blame them, not us. And me and Zak knew Kale and Dandy from school, though they was in the year below us. They was hanging about getting their collar felt for nicking motors and burgling. We decided to put our heads together and hit the road in a stolen VW Camper van on false plates. We would tour towns, looking for rich pickings with good escape routes and bad CCTV coverage.

We also did a quick recce on the bad boys of the manor too – some places you don't mess about in, know what I mean?

Our first job went tits-up big style.

It was in an up-market jeweller's in Camden Town. Dandy was the doorman, turned the sign around so it read 'closed' from the outside, and stood against it so it wouldn't open. Kale was in the car waiting around the corner, and me and Zak were front of house, if ya like. We didn't use proper weapons back then. There was some kind of unspoken rule that said if you went in with guns, you'd kind of crossed a line, see? Hammers and bats and the like were our choice back then. If you got collared by the law, you could reckon on a good spell indoors, but if you had guns and such, you were going down for a long time, coming out when you was a fucking pensioner, man. Not worth it.

Anyway, this particular shop was a fucking doddle. Two members of staff, an old woman who wore a monocle and used bulldog clips round the back of her head to tighten up the loose skin on her face – I made that up, don't listen to me – and a young geezer looked like he wanted to be a trainee butler, hoity-toity, nose in the air, black waistcoat, you know what I mean. No CCTV outside, which tends to be better quality than the stuff they stick up in the shops these days; it's Council, see, or it's a cooperative between the Council and the coppers. But inside the stores, it's generally shit quality. It don't bother us anyway, we're hooded and gloved.

This job was something your local amateur youths could take down easy as piss, except it bit us in the arse pretty hard. I went at the displays with a hammer, Zak was screaming at them, scaring the shit out of them, freezing them to the spot, making them… compliant – good word, Nelson! Compliant. I was ramming jewellery into a small black sports bag; I concentrated on rings cos they were usually the most expensive, usually all concentrated in one or two areas under the counters, difficult to damage, and easiest to fence. Leave the watches and the other shit, too much hassle. In and out, that's our motto.

Except, when my bag was full, I looked up because Zak's shouting had changed in tone from threatening to pleading. I couldn't work out what had happened at first, but then I saw the fucking butler had Zak's arm up his back and the old dear had one of them ring gauges – the long metal rods – up against his throat. Except it wasn't just up against his throat, the tip of it was buried *in* his throat – I reckon it was up to J or K, Zak swore it was up to T.

Anyway, it seemed all three were staring at me as though the next move was mine. I suppose it was really, seeing as I was the only one not in a compromising position. If I put down the bag and walked out the door, they would've let Zak go to do the same, see? It was an unspoken understanding.

'Cept I didn't find that compromise all that agreeable.

I zipped up my bag as I walked to the old lass. I could see her name tag pinned to the thin white blouse she wore. Dierdre, it said. "Let 'im go, Dierdre," I said.

"Put that down," she said to me, nodding at the black bag.

"You've got insurance," I said. "Now be a good gal and let 'im go, sit on the fucking floor and no one needs to get hurt, know what I mean?"

It seemed that she didn't know what I meant at all. She pushed the ring gauge further into Zak's neck and his eyes nearly popped out of his fucking face. I put the bag down, and she relaxed her grip a bit. From my jacket pocket, I took a short knife and jabbed it in her eye. Straight through the monocle. Who the fuck did she think she was?

Let me tell you, she let Zak go pretty fucking quick then. Scream? Jesus, she nearly burst my fucking eardrums!

The butler nearly had a heart attack, and Zak was rubbing his throat and almost doubling over with laughter as we reached the door. Yes, I'd picked up the black bag again and was about to turn back and give the butler a swift going over when Dandy shouted the word we all hated to hear: blue.

It meant the coppers were here.

Bitch had hit the button. I didn't think either of them would have had the balls to do that, but she had. I stared at the door, and then I stared at Dierdre and the butler, teeth gnashing together. Dandy came in and dropped the grille door. All three of us hurried to the back of the shop. I grabbed the butler and threw him through the privacy curtain. "Open up the back door and do it now before I stab *you* in the eye."

The butler was fumbling for keys, breathing quick like he was on full-panic mode, but he'd hardly flinched when he had Zak's arm, like it was something he'd practiced for, see? So when he starts breathing like a greyhound, I got a bit panicky myself and punched him in the face. He hit the floor and curled up, so I kicked him while I had the chance. Zak looked out through the peephole in the back door and confirmed that the law was all over the back car park too. Bastards. "I count two," he said.

You ever seen *Heat*? Brilliant film. Anyway, there's how many robbers, four, five? And there's six thousand police, all armed like they was mercenaries – it was obscene. Well, this ain't America, this is li'l old England – no weapons on patrol coppers, armed coppers a fucking week away. And the two coppers out back probably represented about half the total staff of the force. All they had was pepper spray and a stick. Bit pathetic, really. Anyway, I get the butler to his feet and make him open the door. When I peered out, the coppers didn't exactly rush us like the Flying Squad, know what I mean? They held back, nervous, papping themselves, squeaking into their radios.

"Where's your coat?"

He stuttered, "My—"

"Coat. Yes, where's your fucking coat?"

He pointed to a tiny room to my right. In it was a sink and a kettle, little fridge, and a table. On the wall, two jackets. One screamed Dierdre – beige, matching scarf draped over the shoulders. The other was a short sports jacket, black woollen scarf sticking out of the pocket. I grabbed it, made the butler put it on and then put the scarf around his face, tied it tight at the back of his head, and found a pair of gloves – one in each pocket, aw bless.

Zak grinned at me, and Dandy grabbed him by the neck, almost lifted him off his feet. "Walk out there," he said. "And you tell them there's eight of us in here, okay? Tell them we're armed with shotguns, and we're fucking crazy, okay?"

He was nodding like his head was going to fall off, and honestly, I was struggling to keep from laughing – you know those tense situations where all you want to do is laugh your tits off? Yeah, well that was me then.

The butler trips over the back doorstep and walks out up the narrow path and into a kind of courtyard where this shop and those either side take their deliveries. He's got his hands in the air as though there are six thousand guns pointing at him, and he's screaming, "I work here, I work here, don't shoot."

He gets about twenty yards into the courtyard, and the two coppers exchange glances – funny as fuck to see. They see this geezer with a face mask and gloves on claiming he works there, coming out of the back of a jeweller's that's just been turned over, and they yell at him to get on the floor.

I nearly fell over right there and then, it was hilarious.

Well, we didn't wait for no invitation. As soon as they both hurried over to the butler who was on his knees, we legged it out the back, did a sharp right and tried the door of the next shop along. It opened and the heat hit us. We went in and it turned out to be a hairdresser's gaff. All the blowers on full blast, it was like walking into a fucking sauna, man. Anyway, we walked straight through the shop, and straight out the front door, bold as you like. We turned left and left again, and there was Kale, leaning against the car having a smoke, *Bat Out of Hell* leaking from an open window. "Everything alright?" he said.

Good days. We learned a lot. We learned a lot about ourselves and about each other – especially that we looked out for each other. No one ever bottled it and left anyone behind. Well, they did, but only once. And we had no choice.

That one time happened at another jeweller's in fucking Chelsea of all places. Yeah, you think you know what you're doing and trying to get better every time you do a job, but sometimes, you fucked up and made a series of bad calls, ended up in shit at roughly shoulder level.

We did the same this time as we always did: Kale in the car nearby, Dandy was looking after the doors, and me and Zak went in shouting and screaming – I always liked that approach; if people think you're nutters, they're likely to cooperate, know what I mean?

We'd grown more sophisticated too, and we each wore them earpieces you see coppers wearing. It wasn't just for show, we was only on a fucking conference call, wasn't we? Wonderful! Kale was keeping his peepers open while we was inside doing the job. And it turned out to be a fucking lifesaver this one time. The balloon had gone up and we was none the wiser – another silent alarm thing. We'd bagged some good stuff and was aiming for the door when blue came over the air.

Me and Dandy made it out while Zak had been making a mess of this kid's face – another butler type of kid – and the rest of the staff had fled out the back door, weeing their knickers. As we walked calmly away from the shop, I heard Kale shouting to Zak to stay put, stay put! He had a good view of the front of the shop where we was, and of the entrance to the back of the shop too. And he said there was filth out back with the staff members. And if he was going to walk out the front, he'd get nabbed by another pair of coppers who'd just pulled up.

He was trapped.

So he hid.

We thought they'd put the dogs in there to search but they didn't! Couldn't believe it – shoddy police work, that. Anyway, here's a tip we were going to put into action some time. We was told that if you carry a small squirty bottle of dog piss with you, and you end up being trapped like that, spray it around everywhere and it'll put the dogs off your scent and you're in the clear. I could never bring myself to follow a dog round and trying to get it to piss in a bottle though. Some things are not worth the aggro.

Anyway, Zak hid in a hallway closet that was full of boxes and bags and rubbish, burying himself. The coppers didn't find him! Couldn't believe it! Anyway, after a couple of hours, when the coppers had left, we told Zak he was in the clear, and he was able to smash a window and get the hell out. That's why we got the earpieces, so we could keep in touch if anything went tits-up. I always wondered what would have happened if he was discovered. Scares the shit out of me, does that. If it was me… yeah, I would kill someone to get away. I really would.

Think about it; if I got caught and they pinned all them armed robberies on me, I would go down for life. But if I take someone out, I've got a reasonable chance of legging it, see? If I get caught for snuffing someone, I ain't going to get a much longer sentence than I would've got just for the robberies. No incentive, see? So I might as well top someone and take my chances.

Zak declared he had claustrophobia or something in that small cupboard. It messed with his head, he said. Kale was itching to get his hands dirty, so we swapped 'em both. Zak became a driver, and things seemed to run a lot smoother for us from then on.

Another piece of kit we always used these days was a parked car. No, not the one Zak was sitting in, another one, close to the job. It would be legit in that it was taxed and tested, insured too. Before each job, we'd park it up and leave the keys under the driver's seat; it was risky, but it never got nicked. We'd never needed to use it, but everyone agreed it was a good idea to have a safety net, and so since then, we always brought our spare car along.

We'd done a few jobs around Bermondsey, and the noise on the streets was the coppers were putting together a team to try and nail us. Don't get me wrong, that was kind of flattering, if you see what I mean. But if it was a choice of being flattered or staying out of the big house, then we'll exit stage left with red faces and tails between our legs – it ain't no problem. Stay free, man. Well, we had a sit-down in a pub one night, and decided to break free from London altogether. We pointed the van north and after two hundred miles, landed in Leeds.

Most of it seemed like any other big city, seventy percent shithole, and thirty percent glitz. Yeah, it'll do, we thought. It was plenty big enough for us to stretch our legs and really get to grips with things. We'd made a play down south for Post Offices and up here in Leeds we saw no reason to change. Zak selected our targets with care, never rushing. We'd learned that Leeds had a network of cameras on big black poles, and the coppers called it Leeds Watch – I fucking love Google. They even tell you where they are. You subtract those locations from the locations of the bigger Post Offices and instantly you've got yourself a decent list of targets.

The ones we was interested in were those near fairly big shops and restaurants cos they would cash up the takings and hand them in to the Post Office. Bingo – easy pickings and fat pickings too. We'd been here five or six months, staying in separate digs and only meeting when we were planning a job or doing a job. We figured it was the safest way forward.

Each of us knew that the longer we did this shit for the more likely it was we'd end up getting caught. We ain't stupid. So we took precautions, and if I'm honest, the more precautions we took, the less this lifestyle appealed to me. Don't get me wrong, I still got a big kick out of taking down a job and walking away eighty-grand richer. But it could only last so long before our luck ran out, see?

We was getting tired, I think. All of us. Zak was turning into a slumped shoulders kind of guy, and I think he was weakening. We needed some time off.

I don't know. I had some plans of my own bubbling underneath the surface, know what I mean? I had thought about going solo, but as yet, nothing came to mind.

As a team, we planned to see the year out in Leeds and then hop over the Pennines to Manchester, do a year there and then bail the country.

I hadn't been dumb with my split. I'd divided it into three piles: one pile went into a safety deposit box – I had one in the NatWest Bank in Windsor, and now I had another at Santander in Leeds, and I paid three grand each month into a business account at Lloyds – my cover was a self-employed builder, pay tax and national insurance, the works. See, not thick as pigshit, eh? And I kept a decent wad put by as petty cash. I know Zak had a similar setup. We kept each other's account details in case one of us pegged it.

I reckoned I had nearly eight hundred grand, and I'd quit when I reached a mill. Ha, I say that now, but I know what I'm like – I'll probably carry on. Remember *Butch Cassidy and the Sundance Kid*? Yeah, cool flick, man. They had more than enough cash, but they couldn't stop robbing banks, and I know why. It had nothing to do with greed, really. It becomes a way of life, and if you stop doing it, you look around wondering what else life has to fucking offer. And if you like a thrill, then pickings were pretty slim. So you fell back on what you knew best: robbing.

Anyway, that was the plan. But it changed as autumn turned to winter. I was flitting from a cheap and shitty hotel to a cheap and shitty bed and breakfast. I changed locale roughly every three weeks – I don't like people getting used to me, see? I don't like people getting familiar cos then they start asking questions and digging into your private life, and I only ever share that shit with the crew.

Yeah, things changed, alright. And her name was Shannon. We got together as a result of her rolling her car into the back of mine at a Starbucks drive-thru. Yeah, romantic, eh? Anyway, we parked up and swapped details. I didn't intend taking it any further because there was no damage to my motor, and I ain't telling no one who the hell I am. But she insisted we swap details – especially phone numbers. She didn't get no details, but I gave her a phone number. And things developed from there.

I never felt totally comfortable with her. We was no Bonnie and Clyde, know what I mean? At the end of the first month she told me where she worked, and I almost shit a brick. I thought it was a set-up at first, that she was out to spy on me. But I could see in her eyes that she had no idea I was anything other than a self-employed builder who travelled around the country looking for work.

No one else in the crew had a bird. If they were desperate, they quickly learned where the red-light areas were. But I had my own woman now, and things were getting twitchy – Zak especially didn't like the idea. He said he left his woman back in Walford to concentrate on this life. We argued for a few days, almost coming to blows over it. It wouldn't be the first time the crew had bloodied their fists on one of their own – it happened, fellas working close together all that time, bound to happen.

I sulked for a couple of weeks, and the crew went about their regular business of sussing the places around Leeds for a decent target.

Eventually, me and Zak made up. I realised he was right, and I was wrong, and let me tell ya, it takes a proper man to know when he's wrong, and it takes a man with balls to own up to it. I owned up to it. There. Job first, live your life second.

Shannon told me where she worked – police. She said she worked in the personnel department looking after timecards and annual leave requests and shit like that. But really, in the police is *in the police*, know what I mean? Yep. Imagine how my heart nearly fell out through my arse when she said that. I suppose if she wasn't a spy – and I honestly don't think she was – I could have gauged her, maybe turned her and used her as a spy. But really, who the hell am I kidding? That's the kind of shit you watch on telly; people don't go spying on policing tactics and then run and tell their robber boyfriend and his robbing friends, do they? And anyway, this is where another thing came into play. As I was considering this, she was holding my hand, and she looked at me and said, "You're not a builder, Nelson. Are you?"

I didn't know where to look. I fronted her out, telling her of course I was, and I even came out with a load of building terms I'd picked up from college in the hopes it would convince her.

It didn't work. She just stared at me. "Your hands are smoother than mine."

Ah. Yep, caught hook, line, and whatever else they say. I pulled my hand away pretty quick. And then I said, "It's over, Shannon."

"So what do you do?"

I said nothing. What the hell could I say?

"It's okay," she said. "You can trust me."

"Trust you? What with?"

She shrugged. "I mean, if it's not totally legal." She stared at me. "I could… I mean I might be able to help out. Just saying."

"Help out? With what?" This was turning into a game of you show me yours and I'll show you mine. Well, Nelson don't show his tackle to no one first.

"Information."

I smiled at her, hoping she'd open up a bit more and tell me what she thought she knew about me. Right then that was the only information I wanted from her. We was a very successful outfit because we planned our shit meticulously, and we kept ourselves to ourselves. I wasn't about to take no fucking chances now. I suppose that was a rash response: we could always use info about coppers and what was going on in their filthy heads, what they knew about us.

But I thought about it for a moment longer. I'd be stupid to turn this down. I closed right in on her, and I must've come across as threatening, but I was just being cautious – you never know who's earwigging. "Tell me what you know about me."

She tried to draw back but I grabbed her by the coat and held her there just a couple of inches away from me.

"You're hurting me."

"Tell me. What do you know?"

"Nelson, I… I don't know anything yet. I've only just thought of asking you. I don't know anything about you. If I knew more about you, then I'd be able to check things out at work."

I squinted. "If you knew what?"

"Your real name. Your mates' real names. What you're into."

I bit my bottom lip – not in a seductive way, either. I was trying to focus my mind, remove any emotion and keep things logical, and pain helped me to do that. I looked into her eyes, searching for that speck of betrayal that most people have there. I couldn't see one. But come on, what the hell did that prove?

I'd known her just a month or two, and here I was considering putting my own freedom and the freedom of my entire crew – who have known each other for many successful years – in danger. What the hell was I thinking about? I was being a mug.

For a moment, I considered putting her lights out. But if I did that, I'd get my collar felt in the morning. And if I did that, the whole operation would crumble and that would be it, game over. And if I went even further and took her out of the equation altogether, I was banking on us not already being under surveillance, wasn't I? I was banking on her not having a finger or two in my own file sitting on some police inspector's desk waiting for an update from her. If I topped her, and we was under investigation, they'd definitely feel my collar in the morning.

"Shannon, I don't know what you think I'm up to, and what you think you know about any of my friends – and I don't have any, really. But you're so far up the wrong tree that you're in the wrong fucking post code, love." I stood up. "Okay? I am a self-employed building consultant," I brushed her cheek with my fingertips. "I look after my skin – building work is for plebs. I have my own consultancy, okay?"

I wanted to look around, sure we was being watched. I have never felt so uncomfortable with someone. I walked away and didn't look back.

"Nelson. Nelson, please!" I could hear her crying in the dark. I closed the door and forgot all about her. Crew first, this kind of shit second. Actually, a lot lower than second. It was in the thousands.

No idea what happened to her after that.

Didn't matter anyway, the crew had something that would take my mind off women completely. Zak had found a nice little Post Office job – eighty to one-hundred grand potential. I had an idea this might be our last job.

PART THREE

Chapter Five

The Scene

ALTHOUGH IT SAID POST Office outside, you could have been walking into any one of thousands of newsagents across the country. In fact, no you couldn't, because to the right as you walked in was a deli counter too. You had two or three aisles up the centre of the shop with shelves stacked high with everything from crisps and nuts to tins of spaghetti and packets of rice. To the left was the newsagent and stationery department – everything from *The Telegraph* to crossword puzzles, soft porn at the top, with BBC and motoring magazines lower down, competing for space with highlighter pens and padded envelopes.

The bank of curved glass display units on the far right were largely empty, but I reckoned through daylight hours they'd be packed with sausage rolls, pork pies, quiches, and samosas, bhajis, that kind of thing. And up by the counter would be doughnuts and cookies and such.

My stomach was rumbling already.

So, if you're standing, as I was, just inside the doors staring straight ahead along the centre aisle, you'd see a counter running left to right across the shop. The counter was maybe four feet high, loaded with lottery displays and another low row of sweet displays. At the far left side was a till, and an open door. From here I could see the edge of the doorframe and light spilling out from the room, but I couldn't see into the room itself.

To the right of the counter was another till and then a corridor that led into the back rooms, I presumed.

Behind the counter was racking loaded with cigarettes and bottles of booze – you've seen this scenario a thousand times, it never changes; it becomes boring – every day you walk into the office knowing there's going to be a ram raid or a burglary where the offenders have smashed their way in to grab all that lovely tobacco from behind the counter because it costs a fucking fortune to buy. I could understand their logic.

Hell, some shop owners even had padlocked shutter doors over that stock, but these bastards would come in with axes or with bolt croppers or just plain old sledge hammers, determined to get their hands on thousands of pounds of gear that they could off-load in the blink of an eye. Who the hell wants to pay a tenner for a packet of fags when you could buy some knocked off fags for a fiver?

"So what's first?"

She made me jump! Jesus, I was fucking miles away. "Photography," I said.

"What about footwear marks?"

I sighed. I already wanted to tell her to fuck off and leave me alone. But I couldn't. She wasn't being rude; she was showing an interest… and she was right. Sort of. It had been raining all afternoon, and the floor was swimming in wet muck – not thick enough to be called mud, but you know what I mean – just a thin layer of damp dirt.

The incident had happened an hour ago – possibly a bit longer, and since then there had been a considerable amount of foot traffic through here, despite the cordon outside. Coppers, gotta love 'em, but they're clumsy as fuck. And I know they have a job to deal with; sometimes forensic work is pushed to the back of the queue, and sometimes it even becomes an afterthought.

The only footwear marks I'd be able to get, if any at all, would be from the counter and possibly from the floor at the staff side beyond the counter – depending on the surface. Out here in the shop, with a hi-grip floor too, footwear marks were a no-go. I explained all this to her, making sure I kept it light-hearted because I was aware that she was still wounded, still emotionally dented.

She shrugged and welled up as though I'd poked her with a stick and laughed at her. "When exactly did you split up with him?"

Her chin wobbled and I thought she was going to collapse into a heap of snot on the floor, but she fanned her face with a hand and tried to smile through it. "Sorry," she said. She swallowed and composed herself. "Fortnight, maybe a bit less."

I nodded. She's had a fortnight to get over this clown and it's affected her like this. I felt like asking if it was true love, but it would have sounded as flippant as it probably was. "How long had you been together?" You see how caring I am? I'm at the scene of an armed robbery, trying to work out my examination sequence, trying to plan ahead, yet here I am engaging in small talk with a snotty tissue about something I couldn't give a sideways shit about. It's all part of my cuddly nature, I can't help myself.

"Three months."

Three months. And after two weeks she's still grief-stricken. What the hell was all that about? Two weeks is plenty of time to get over a three-*year* relationship! Three months equals about twenty-five minutes in my book. But then, what the hell would I know? Job first, all that shit second. Actually, not second – it wasn't even on the same sheet.

Things like this make me look inside myself, at what a blackened shell I am, bereft of any relationship woes, inert, dead.

Just the way I like it.

I looked at Shannon, and thanked God no one took the slightest interest in me, and vice versa. I wanted to scream "Get over it!" But I didn't because I'm not like that.

"I know what you're thinking," she said.

Oh no you fucking don't, I thought.

"I'm such a mess. I never behave like this usually." And then she gritted her teeth, and her eyes slitted up and anger turned her fingers into claws. "I could fucking kill him."

Well I didn't expect that. "You'll get over it, kid," I said. "Stop being so hard on yourself. Give yourself time to heal, eh?"

"Honestly, if I see him again, I'll murder him."

I nodded in thought. This isn't healthy, I also thought. But I countered with this: if I'd killed everyone I'd wanted to kill, there would be about forty-six people left in Leeds. Maybe forty-seven at a push. I understood where she was coming from. "Shall we get on?"

She pulled herself together – yeah, yeah, she was a pair of curtains – get over it. She smoothed herself down as though ready to rock 'n roll without thinking about the loser boyfriend shit.

"Photography first," I said.

And it was. I rattled off ten or fifteen shots inside the shop just to get the layout nailed. These images would be used in briefings (shudder) and perhaps used later in interviews with witnesses or suspects. They had to be good, and I made sure they were.

I was keen to get to the far side of the counter where Ramsay had been attacked. From there I'd be able to see the counter top a little more clearly, and try to work out from the disturbance up there how the offender or offenders had got over it, and how they'd got back over as they fled.

The safest way up there, I thought, was to take a right turn up the back of the deli counter but there was a hand mark in blood on the low swinging door leading to it. I reckoned it would be Ramsay's blood: there were four fingers this side and a thumb on the other side, indicating it had been opened from that side.

"Be aware of this blood," I said to Shannon as I pushed open the deli door.

"You not going to sample it?"

"Sample it? Do you mean swab it? No, I'm not; not yet anyway – depends." It also said to me that it wasn't the offender's blood because they'd have jumped back over the counter and run through the store the same way they'd come in. Sixty-year-old Ramsay wouldn't have jumped the counter, especially if he'd just been attacked.

"What about Ramsay?"

I walked up behind the deli display, camera swinging around my neck, sweat collecting inside the gloves I wore. "What about him?"

"He's a scene, isn't he?"

My eyes widened a bit there. "Yes, he is." I was surprised. "He is indeed. And he'll have his clothing seized."

"How about DNA from his hands?"

"Nope. His hands are contaminated by his own blood." But I appreciated her input now; she was thinking, and she was coming up with some good stuff. "But I like your logic. Keep going." At the end of the walkway, we came to a junction of sorts. Straight ahead was the corridor that led to the back door, and possibly other rooms off to the left of it. To my left was the staff side of the counter, one till within reach, the other at the far end of the counter by the open safe room door.

Now, my eyesight is far from perfect, so I was squinting, but it looked to me as though there was a shitload of cash in the little room, scattered on the floor like a rich-man's carpet.

I made a mental note to photograph my approach to that room, paying attention to any cash I found. I work for the police, and I dare say that me and my colleagues are beyond reproach – we are trusted, and we trust each other. But the public and our Professional Standards Directorate aren't quite so trusting. No way would I throw my career away for a few grand, but they don't know that, and so I would photograph my approach and then collect the cash and get an inspector to book it into the safe once back at the nick. If I didn't have Shannon as a witness, I'd consider getting a copper from outside to come and witness me collecting the dosh – everyone's happy then.

But before then, there was the counter and the floor to examine.

This had been the site of a frenzied attack. I know that term is thrown around the media like confetti at a wedding, but this really was frenzied. Crushed packets of cigarettes, papers, upturned stool, a black plastic till drawer, newspapers that had been dragged from the countertop along with fliers and staplers, pens, all items strewn across this piece of floor. And blood. Lots of blood.

There had been one man standing here fending off two armed males who slashed and stabbed and beat as they leapt over the counter, no doubt screaming and yelling at him. It must have been terrifying.

The floor was carpet, and I suppose if you spent all day on your feet behind a counter, you'd want a decent carpet to walk on. It was thick and it was pale, showing up the blood splashes and patterns easily enough. Nothing worse than trying to photograph blood on a fucking red carpet – if you intend getting stabbed, please don't buy red carpets!

Shannon was right behind me as I photographed my way along the floor; flash bouncing off the ceiling to diffuse the light, wide angle lens picking out the floor, the shelves to the right full of booze that gave way to those large nylon sacks in metal frames that fill up with letters and parcels throughout the day, and those to the left under the counter: spare till rolls, clipboards of invoices or delivery sheets, I don't know. The two tills, the far one open, blood across the drawer worthy of its own scaled image. I'd swab that one later, along with, perhaps the blood on the low deli door.

On the floor below the open till drawer was a wad of paper spilling from a split envelope. On the envelope was a footwear impression. My heart raced just a little bit more – and I'm aware of how sad that makes me sound, but this is forensic evidence left behind by an offender. It was like suddenly discovering you were in the chase, you were on the track of justice, dragging behind you the investigation and the interviews and the court case – everything in the wake of this – a fucking envelope that some idiot had stood on. This was a rush.

I photographed the footwear impression using oblique lighting right across the envelope, complete with a forensic scale to one side, labelled appropriately with my designated exhibit number. I then seized the envelope, tapping the papers the rest of the way out and leaving them on a shelf under the till. And that was when all my birthdays came at once. I love jobs like these.

"What?" asked Shannon, trying to peer over my shoulder as I squatted down and then knelt.

"A balaclava." Unlike the confetti at the wedding, this thing stood out like a fresh turd on the top table. If I'd thought the footwear mark on the envelope was good, this was gold! It would give a name – even if there were no hairs inside. Of course, the ultimate is that it has hairs inside, hairs with bulbs so you can load those onto the DNA database, where the machine will spit a name out at you along with your commendation and a certificate of awesomeness. But even if there are no hairs, they can still scoop user DNA – it's still a bullseye, and I was destined to leave this scene a very happy man, giving good news to my CID colleagues along the way.

With the balaclava recorded and seized, and now sitting inside a sealed paper evidence bag on the shop floor in front of the deli counter, I could begin examining the counter for footwear marks.

I know, I've already found one – that I believe belongs to an offender – so why do I need to examine the counter for more? Well, so far, I've only put one offender at the staff side of the counter, and I wanted to put them both there. If there was no CCTV to go on after all, I wanted to solidify the number of offenders, and I wanted to hang a story, a theory, around their necks before they went into interview. I had to consider their possible defence: it wasn't me, I went into the shop to buy Polos, but I didn't go over the counter. Honest, guv.

The first thing I did was clear a section of counter near the right hand till that hadn't been involved in the attack. The second thing I did was climb up onto it and stomp around a bit. I could use this piece of countertop – much like a kitchen counter – to determine what powder, if any, gave good results. I had a choice of black globular, white globular (my favourite), or good old-fashioned aluminium flake.

Sometimes none of them worked; instead of enhancing contamination – which is all a footwear mark is – they obliterated it. In that case, you're working with a black gelatine lift with a healthy dose of luck thrown in too. And sometimes, even that would fail. If you've got so far down that avenue, you're looking at enhanced photography or exotic powders or even chemical treatment to bring out the detail. And yes, I would go that far for those footwear marks. I love footwear marks.

I was lucky. White powder worked a treat on my own countertop footwear marks. I powdered up the attacked area and before my eyes, three footwear marks popped up and slapped me in the face. They were quite beautiful, rich in detail, almost complete impressions. My little heart sang.

I was getting well inside this examination now, and I was loving it. I'd almost forgotten that Shannon was even there; she seemed content to observe and interrupted me infrequently, something I was grateful for. When you get inside a scene in your mind as well as your body, it's a good idea to stay there and watch what's going down; picturing the event happening in front of you as though you'd been sitting on the chair all afternoon just waiting for it to happen.

But I saw something that made me sit up and stop labelling and photographing and lifting.

"What's up?"

I stood back and looked at the three footwear marks. Two, a Nike Air and some kind of boot, pointed inward – towards the racks of booze. These were the offenders leaping over the counter, just putting one foot down to make it across. But there was only one footwear mark pointing back into the shop.

"Maybe the second one cleared it in one go?"

I pulled off my gloves and stood there thinking. No, that didn't make sense. The counter was at least three feet across, and this piece of floor on the staff side was maybe two feet across at best. You'd need to be an Olympic athlete to clear the counter in one go. And if you could clear it in one go, why did you need to put your foot down on the initial leap across?

"So they went out by running down the deli path first, and out through the low door."

I nodded, that had to be it. That explained it.

Except it didn't.

I pictured both lads jumping over the counter and beating Ramsay over the head with bats or machetes or whatever. Ramsay goes down, one of them continues to assault him while the other goes through into the safe room and fills a shopping bag. The one who's assaulting Ramsay stops, maybe thinking he's done enough, but Ramsay gets up, furious, and the kid jumps over the counter and heads for the door, calling his mate to follow him. Ramsay can't leap the counter, and he runs down the deli aisle and out into the shop.

"Leaving one man in here?"

I looked at her, my arms folded, and nodded.

Shannon was shaking her head. "The witness at the petrol station saw the offenders leaving."

"CID said they saw offenders leaving – but they didn't say how many. Did three come in or just two? How many went back out? The witness saw three people leaving, but was one of them Ramsey? And can you trust a witness, anyway?" I looked at my watch and was surprised to see it was just gone eight o'clock already. I still had so much to do, and CID would be here in less than an hour.

She came closer, ducked her head down a bit. "You saying one of them is still here?"

"I'm not saying that, no." I was thinking it though. "I'm saying I can't account for one of them. Yet."

"You're scaring me."

I put on some fresh gloves and photographed the safe room prior to entering.

It was tiny. There was a small desk with a chair in front of it, drawers everywhere, full of postal forms and stickers, books and books of postage stamps. Above the desk were more shelves, this time loaded with plastic boxes of coins and scratch cards. There was a small safe under the desk, door wide open, dregs of cash left on the shelves inside. The other side of the room, still within a few feet of the desk, was another safe, this one five-feet high – door wide open, only a few tubs of bagged pound coins still there.

On the floor, again carpeted, were wads of cash. Thousands of pounds in tens and twenties. If Ramsay lived through the night, you could bet your arse his bosses at the Post Office would kill him tomorrow.

I checked the cash for footwear impressions but found none. And rather than collect it all, I decided the best way of dealing with it would be to shove it all in the safe room, lock the door, and hand the key to CID when they showed up.

I did all that and walked the length of the counter back towards till number two, and that's when I stopped dead. Now *I* was frightened.

"Eddie?"

"Sssshhh," I said. I stared at Shannon, my eyes wide enough to hurt, and whispered, "Can you hear that?"

She went pale. "No, what?"

"I could hear a tinny kind of voice."

"A what?"

I shook my head. Maybe I was imagining it.

PART FOUR

Chapter Six

The Groupie

I COULDN'T HELP MYSELF. I said to myself, "Shannon, grab him with both hands!"

Ever since the first day I met him – in a Starbucks car park – I've known that he was the man for me. He wasn't the best-looking man I'd ever seen, not by a long way. But he had something that none of the others had: he had presence, and he had something I struggle even now to put my finger on; I think it's something like selfishness but it's not quite, if you see what I mean.

He knows what he wants, and he goes balls-out to get it.

He told me, over the course of the next few weeks, that he was a builder and I saw no reason to suspect otherwise – I always thought he was being honest with me. He had a wonderful southern accent that held me captive, and I just wanted to be with him every minute of every day.

And the days when we were apart turned me into some kind of rubber woman – wait, that sounds completely wrong! Not a rubber woman, as such. I mean I was turned to jelly; I was useless, couldn't concentrate on anything, and was practically paralysed until the next time I saw him. And this was a regular thing – I only came to life when we were together. Yes, I'm aware how pathetic that sounds. I've never been a romantic, but it only takes being with one person, the person you're meant to be with, to change how you look at life and how your brain functions.

I work for the police as a personnel officer. It's a shit job no matter how glamourous it might sound. I look after timecards for officers and staff and I monitor our computer programs to make sure time off and annual leave has been correctly implemented. And I take internal calls from those officers and staff and I become their doormat as they vent their anger at me.

I hate my job.

I always thought I'd join the force just so I could jump into CSI one day. I always fancied wearing those white suits and going into murder scenes and... well, whatever it is they do. I longed for the status, I suppose, maybe the glamour too – that job really is glamourous!

I know there's a long queue to get in there, but I had the advantage over most of those who'd apply for a CSI role – I worked with the police already, had been through vetting and knew the structure, the procedures, and the policies. All I had to do was book some time with CSI as an attachment and it would bump my application up another couple of levels.

When I met Nelson all thoughts of a stupid fucking career vaporised.

And it was inevitable that we'd get around to talking about careers. That particular conversation happened a lot later than I expected it to. He seemed content to be with me whoever I was and wherever I worked. But it happened one day. I bit the bullet and told him I worked for the police as a pen-pusher. I emphasised I was office-based, and it wasn't as a police officer... but I saw him take a step backwards from me; not physically, but you can just tell when someone wants to distance themselves and quickly. I felt like a leper. And worse than that, I felt like I'd already lost him.

"Listen," I'd said, "you're not a builder. I know you're not a builder cos your hands are smoother than mine." I smiled again, wider, trying to reassure him that it was okay he'd lied, I understood, that I knew he was no nine-to-five suit-wearing accountant; I knew he was spending time on the wrong side of the law, and that just made the whole thing even more thrilling for me. Forget being in the police, forget getting a job with CSI; none of that shit was a match for being with Nelson. I felt alive! I wanted to be a part of his world. I didn't want to be a part of this world.

I forget how it went exactly, but he came in real close and he grabbed my coat. "Tell me what you know about me," he said.

Well, I didn't know anything about him! Not through the police, I mean. I knew he was a southerner, but that was about all. I had no idea he wanted to know what the police held on him – I didn't fucking know, did I? "Tell me your real name, your mates' names and what you're into, and I might be able to find something out for you." I shrugged as best I could under the circumstances.

After that, he let me go, but I could tell right then that we were finished. If I'd noticed him take a psychological step back before, this time he didn't take a step back, he took a flight to Mars. It was a very sad time in my life, and though it feels like it happened last year, it only happened last week, and I feel raw and very emotional; I'd do anything to get back with him.

Time has a way of messing with your head when you don't care about it, when you don't notice it passing by because you're too wrapped up in the present.

This attachment with CSI was the only thing I had to look forward to.

My time with Nelson was dead, so I picked up the remnants of my old existence and tried to make it work. He was okay, this guy called Eddie Collins. He tried to come across as a hard bastard, but I could see through the disguise; he was soft as shit – and I mean that as a compliment. Underneath the tough man exterior was a nice man inside. We had a smoke together and he tried to cheer me up, but I was still in a right state over Nelson.

"You need to find some fucking dignity," Eddie told me. "You were dumped by someone who's going through life as a bottom-feeder leaching off other people until he's eventually shot dead or locked up for life. Is that who you want to hook up with?"

And that was like a slap in the face. At first, I thought he was just a cheeky bastard – how dare he say something like that to me after I'd spent all evening crying to him about Nelson. But he was right. Nelson didn't trust me, and he'd treated me very badly. Who's to say what would have happened if we had got together, I could have ended up as a battered wife, or worse. I shuddered.

But a part of me hoped we would have ended up like Bonnie and Clyde. It was romantic.

Eddie turned out to be as enthusiastic about his job as I'd imagined Nelson to be about his. We buzzed around a couple of burglaries this evening, and I couldn't quite get over how thorough he was, how tolerant of people who were blubbing and crying every bit as much as I had. These people were upset because someone had broken into their homes and stolen irreplaceable things from them.

I found the scenes to be enlightening – yes, I could do this job, and I'd be as good as Eddie was. I'd be as thorough, and I'd be the hero that these people saw him to be – and I found them upsetting too. How these people had come home from a hard day at work only to find that some scumbag thought they deserved the victim's cash or heirlooms more than they did. Eddie was furious about them and didn't hold back – it was always those who worked hard for the things they had, or suffered for them, that ended up being victims. It was never the fucking scumbags, was it?

And as those words fell off the end of Eddie's tongue, my mind slipped across to Nelson again. Was he a scumbag who burgled people? Surely not. No, Nelson wouldn't do that sort of thing – that was low, wasn't it, and Nelson wasn't low – he had scruples, he had morals!

And here we were at an armed robbery at a Post Office of all places.

It was horrific; it really was. Two men had jumped over a counter and beaten the postmaster with machetes and bats or whatever, and almost killed him. I was horrified, and I tasted sick in my mouth, a bit of bile in the back of my throat at the sight of all that blood behind the counter.

I tried to imagine that this scene was my scene. I imagined myself doing all the things that Eddie was doing and scoring myself against him. I wasn't doing too well. I tried to follow his logic and work out his methodology, but I was at a loss as to how he was thinking through his processes. I felt like an intruder every time I asked him something. He was so deep into the scene that it was like waking someone up from a deep sleep where they were clearly having a good time in a dream.

Would I have a good time like Eddie was having? I don't think so. I don't think I could ever see this life, this CSI life, as anything other than a job.

I saw the floor of the safe room. There must have been twenty thousand quid there. Eddie didn't even look twice at it. I did. I looked and I let my imagination loose, spending it all on Prada and holidaying in…

I think on balance I would have preferred to see how far I got riding the Nelson horse than I would riding the CSI horse – assuming I ever made it into the CSI stable in the first place. I slipped away into a daydream as Eddie messed about in the safe room. And I was wondering what it would be like to be a part of Nelson's gang – assuming he had a gang. Did he work alone? Was he a burglar? What did he do? Corporate theft? Vehicle crime?

Eddie came towards the till and his face sent me cold. His eyes were wide, and he was staring into nothing, like he was a million miles away. I was getting frightened. "Eddie?"

"Sssshhh," he said. "Can you hear that?"

I couldn't hear anything. "No, what?"

"I could hear a tinny kind of voice."

"A what?"

You know when your fingers tingle and you suddenly go all cold as the blood drains away? I was feeling like that. I was so far over the edge that I thought I would fall off and faint any second. I could actually feel my heart thudding in my chest. I couldn't believe what happened next.

PART FIVE

Chapter Seven

The Door

I COULD SEE THE colour draining from Shannon's face. Her eyes widened, and she looked over her shoulder, checking where the exit was in case she needed it quickly. That whole series of reactions was derived from my own demeanour, because until now I couldn't account for one of the gang members.

That changed in an instant.

I saw a tiny piece of a footwear mark. You've seen those universal work boot patterns a million times – the ones with ribs around the outside of the sole and a series of four-point stars in the middle? In the corridor near the second till were three of those stars and a couple of ribs too. And the impression was in blood. It was a significant find. It was a scary find – potentially.

I nodded at the marks. They stood out to me like someone had installed a neon light in the floor. She looked down for a minute. She looked up at me again, and her eyebrows said she hadn't a clue what I was talking about.

She shrugged, "What?"

I pointed and tried but failed to hide the sigh. "There. Footwear mark in blood."

Again she looked at me, a crooked smile and puppy eyes said she still couldn't see it. I had to fucking bend and practically stick my finger in it.

She gasped, "Oh! A footwear mark."

It took a lot of restraint, but I didn't applaud, nor did I cheer or offer a high-five. I was tempted though.

"What does it mean?"

My turn to look confused. My mouth fell open. "It's a fucking… Shannon. It's the same mark as the one on the counter. The one that's coming in, but not going out again?"

"So you think…?"

I nodded. "Possibly." I looked down a narrow, dark corridor into a dark room at the end. If this had been a normal house, I'd be looking through into the kitchen and the wall facing me would be where the back door was.

The hallway was maybe fifteen yards long, and then there was the doorframe to the black 'kitchen'. I followed the bloody footwear mark up the corridor, watching as each subsequent mark was fainter than its predecessor. I flicked the torch on, bent as I shuffled along, and I got as far as that doorframe before I realised the pattern hadn't repeated for three or four paces.

Strange.

I reached forward and bent my arm around into the black room and turned on the light. Not a single window in sight. A couple of fridges hummed over in the corner. Concrete floor, a row of red fire extinguishers. Boxes, shelves, bottles of everything from booze to vinegar and Irn Bru lined one wall. Next was a small counter with a sink buried in it, a microwave, some mugs, and a coffee jar with a brown-stained teaspoon next to it. In the far wall was indeed a back door, a thick metal bar dropped into hooks in the doorframe, alarm contacts on the top corner, a mortice making sure this thing stayed closed.

I turned around and noted how Shannon hadn't moved. She was still standing by the second till, and it looked as though she hadn't taken a breath in the last twenty minutes. She was ready to explode with fear. I walked slowly back up the corridor, just a couple or three short stutter paces that ended at a door to my right. I turned out the torch, noted how there was no light seeping out from under it or from around the sides.

"Be careful." She was practically eating her fists.

I reached for the handle and she screamed.

Chapter Eight

The Switch

I SWUNG THE DOOR open and blackness hit me only moments before the gun did. The pain exploded in my head. I saw rows of blinking green and red lights and among them all I saw tiny white pinpricks of light dancing in my vision. I always thought that seeing stars was just a piece of shit they used in cartoons, but nope, it's fucking true.

Something quite strange happened to me then that I never would have expected in a million years. If I'd sat down and thought about what my next act would be, I would have gone through a dozen 300-page notebooks before I got anywhere near. Turns out that I, that sack-of-shit Eddie Collins, had some kind of self-preservation mechanism. Except it was a little different to everyone else's. My self-preservation mechanism didn't drag me out of that room and out of the shop door into the safety of half a dozen bored coppers.

No, my self-preservation mechanism didn't involve me at all. It just shrugged its shoulders and dropped me like a hot potato – off you go, lad, it squealed and pissed off, leaving me to fend for myself. Luckily, and this all happened inside a microsecond, anger took pity on me and pulled me up by the scruff of the neck. And believe me, even *I'm* afraid of my anger. Between us, me and anger ploughed into the bastard until all three of us hit a desk against the wall, scattered whatever might have been on it in all directions.

Someone, I'm guessing it was Shannon, flicked the lights on and I squinted as I threw a punch into some stranger's face. He was like a flabby Michael Keaton but with a decent bit of muscle in his arms. She screamed, confirming it was her standing in the doorway shitting her pants. I took a punch to the gut and doubled up, coughing up nothing as a boot came at my face. I didn't close my eyes; instead I watched it coming at me in slow motion, and I could see Ramsay's blood in the laces and the stitching. I deflected the foot with an elbow and then smashed my fist into Keaton's balls.

The satisfaction I got from feeling his knackers crunch together was wonderful, and I quickly followed it with another punch under his chin. I can still see his eyes screwed shut in pain, teeth on show, blood between them. His head whipped back, and he dropped the gun as I buried another punch to his guts. There was a black wire coming out of his t-shirt collar, and I followed it to see an earpiece draped across his face. It was squeaking but I couldn't make out actual words.

I kicked the gun out of the room and stood up, leaning over him and ready to resume the attack if needed. I was panting like a dog, and there was a buzz like electricity hurtling around my body like I'd touched a live wire. My face felt warm and wet and sure enough my fingertips came away red. Blood was dripping onto my shirt and then onto the floor from the head wound.

We were in an office. Much bigger than the safe room but nowhere near as big as the kitchen back there. Under the bench were rows of flickering red and green lights – it was the CCTV hard drive and Keaton there had attempted to remove them – there were wires hanging out all over the place.

Now I knew why he was in here.

The balaclava I'd found behind the counter was his. It'd come off in the assault on Ramsay. He'd bared his face to the cameras and so while his accomplice hopped back over the counter, Keaton here decided the best course of action was to destroy the CCTV or at least take the hard drive. He did a good job of finding it, but then the world closed its doors on him, and he was trapped.

And I was about to find out exactly what that felt like.

I grabbed him by the arm, forced it up his back and marched him out of the office. I turned us right, towards the shop area, and stopped dead. "What the fuck are you doing?"

Shannon, bless her, had picked up the gun. I'd have preferred her to have kicked it through into the kitchen so it was out of his reach and out of his sight; doing that also meant it would still only have had his DNA on it. But no, she'd fucking picked it up.

"Oi, Clarice Starling, what the fuck do you think you're—"

"Shut up."

"Remember what I said about pliers or screwdrivers that you find at scenes?"

"Shut up, Eddie."

She was in shock; I understood that, so I cut her some slack. "Go and put it on the floor in the safe room, eh?"

I saw a spark in her eyes, and then she smiled a bit and lowered the gun. "Throw me the key."

I pushed Keaton's face into the counter and stood to one side so he couldn't back-kick me, then took out the keys and tossed them to her. I looked away, up at the clock; it said eight-forty. Twenty minutes before the CID superheroes arrived. Never mind, I thought, we have armed coppers out there, they can deal with him; this was an excellent result. "Now, when you've locked up again, go out and get the armed…"

I tried to turn my head and face Shannon again, but I couldn't on account of the gun poking in my face. "Shannon—"

She nudged the barrel.

I swallowed and the strength dribbled out of my muscles. "Look," I said, "I understand how tempting that cash is. But think about it for a minute. It's a bad move, Shann—"

"Let him up."

"What?"

"Move aside, let him go."

"This has gone way past being funny. It's going to look bad on your application, you know that, don't you?"

"Get up, Nelson."

"You know him?" I closed my eyes as a certain realisation settled in for the evening. "He's the boyfriend you were so upset about? You are fucking joking!"

Keaton, or rather Nelson, slid out from under my grasp and stood. He then smashed my face into the counter and more stars prickled the darkness behind my lids. The pain in my face was like the slice of a razor blade right across my forehead, and my eyes watered. I felt like dropping to the floor and hoping they'd just fuck off and leave me alone. But I stood there – stooped there – and listened to them laughing.

"I can't believe it's you."

"I'm a bit shocked m'self, love. I never expected to see you again. I didn't mean to be so rude."

"No, no," she said through a smile, "it's fine. I shouldn't have forced the issue."

I so wanted to shout "Get a room!" But I hate cliché and I also hate pain – he'd have punched me for saying that. Get a cell might have been more appropriate.

"*Now* can I join your gang?" she asked, grinning.

I couldn't believe this. "You planned this?" It was beyond incredible that she should pick the same evening – not day shift, mind – the same *evening* to go out with me on an attachment, the exact same night as a fucked-up robbery where her ex-boyfriend happened to be trapped inside.

"I didn't plan anything, Eddie. Let's call it a happy coincidence, shall we?"

"Are you serious? Happy?"

"Of course you're in, gal!" Nelson grinned too and all I could think of was how happy they both were at my expense. I wanted to throw up. "I'm pleased you were so upset."

She handed him the gun and I just couldn't believe my luck; how long ago was it she said she wanted to kill him? I just closed my eyes and waited. "I am never taking out another attachment."

"Go get the cash," he said to her, and then turned to me. "Where's my bally?"

"Your what?"

"Don't get fucking smart with me, I am double the worst trouble you ever thought of. Now, where's my balaclava?"

"I'll get it," I said, wondering what that shit was all about. "It's just over there." I straightened up, ready to make it onto the shop floor where the coppers who were guarding the scene out front would be able to see me. I hoped.

"Leave it. Shannon, hurry up, love, we 'ave to do one." He fiddled with the wire and with only one hand managed to get the earpiece back in. "You still there, Zak?"

"It'll only take me a minute," I said and began moving.

He kicked my feet from under me and I hit the floor like a sack of shit. That hurts. But when you're not expecting it, it really hurts. I was winded and I smacked my bloody nose on the floor. It hurt so much that I would've screamed if I could have scraped the air into my lungs. As it was, I rolled around a bit thinking of my last exchange with Control: Hit me. I wish I could. If only they could see me now.

My watch said eight-fifty. What was the betting the bastards would show up late?

And right on cue she dropped the bag of cash at his feet like a dog bringing back a ball. "We have to hurry; CID have arranged to be back at nine."

Thanks, Shannon. I hope you grow a third tit. Preferably on your face.

"Go out front," he said to her. "Make sure you collect everything he found. Don't leave nothing behind, gal, okay?"

And she was off. Panting.

Nelson crouched down next to me, and I didn't have to see his face to know he was grinning at me. He jabbed the gun into my ribs. "This is one of the best jobs I've done, sunshine. You know why?"

Wow. The perfect opportunity for a come-back, and I couldn't think of anything to hit him with. Still, did I really want him to stamp on my head? Maybe a blank mind was a good thing then.

"This has been like a game o' bingo. Let me tell you why, eh? We hauled fifty grand, and I reckon we just got another ten or fifteen from the safe room floor. And on top of it all, you ain't got no evidence. At all. Nothing. CCTV don't work, and I just lifted everything you found, see? We got all four corners, and we got a line too."

I sighed; it was true. The only evidence he didn't get was—

"And take the flash card out of his camera, babe."

—the photographs. Sigh.

I wasn't having a very good evening. I'd gone from getting everything including the bullseye, to having nothing but black eyes. Yippee.

He whispered, "There's only one thing stopping us getting the full-house, Eddie."

I didn't respond. It didn't take a fucking genius to work out what that was.

"You."

I was right.

"You're gonna walk us out the back door and along to the end of the lane."

"It's guarded," I blew into the dusty carpet.

"That's why you're going to walk us out, like we're carrying forensic stuff, equipment and whatever."

"Call me simple, but I wonder if you carrying a gun might give the game away a bit."

He laughed and grabbed me by the hair. "You're a cute lad, Eddie, I'll give you that."

I wondered if cute meant the same down south as it did up here. I was even more worried now. "Let me get this straight," I said. "You want me to walk you out so you can kill me once I've got you away from here? Is that right?"

"I ain't gonna kill you, man."

"Really? You don't get the full-house while I can pick you out of a line-up."

He came even closer, practically knelt beside me. "But listen to this. I ain't never killed anyone. I know, I know. I look like a right ol' ruffian, don't I? But it's true, Eddie, I ain't never killed no one. Not yet, anyway," he laughed. "And one thing is guaranteed, my friend, I ain't never done no harm to any copper. God's honest, mate. Never." And he whispered, "But if you don't lead us out of here right now before your pals show up, I will do *her* harm, Eddie, know what I mean? She means nothing to me, she's just a fucking groupie wanting a thrill. If I have to damage her, it won't be pleasant, and she might never recover." He shrugged. "Up to you, mate."

"Is this what you're looking for?"

Nelson left my field of vision, taking his hand off the back of my head. "That's the one, darling. Nice one." He nudged me with his foot. "Eddie's going to walk us all out of here now. Ain't that right, Eddie?"

I got to my feet, stared right at him. He smiled at me, and I looked across to Shannon. She folded her arms, stuck out her hip and smiled at me too. Oh, Shannon, did you ever choose the wrong side. I felt a twinge of bravery surge through me and for a moment I imagined leaping onto Nelson and smashing his face into a pulp. But a combination of things stopped me.

Firstly, there was the gun, and the fact that an armed robber was pointing it at me, and I didn't really trust him to keep to his word – it was always more than just a threat. And there was Shannon. She'd be only too keen to show her 'boyfriend' how loyal she could be. And in my book, two against one isn't especially fair. But the deciding factor in my reluctance to attack Nelson was this: that twinge of bravery was actually a twinge of stupidity dressed up in fancy clothes. Sometimes you couldn't trust yourself to behave honestly, and neither could you trust yourself to behave in your own best interests. Fact of life right there.

I never prayed so hard for CID to arrive at one of my scenes in my life. But if Wilbourne wafted in here on a wave of body odour and poor dress sense, I'd be so glad to see him that I would kiss him – hell, he'd get the tongue as well.

Chapter Nine

The Exit

It didn't happen. Sometimes our prayers are not only ignored, but you can hear someone laughing in the background. After I washed the blood from my face, we found the key to the back door easily enough – it was in the CCTV room on a hook labelled Back Door.

I might have been wrong, but I could have sworn I felt a through draft as we unlocked the back door and swung it wide – seconds later and CID would have been there. I have no idea what might have happened if CID had shown up on fucking time – ha! – and had been presented with an armed robber in the shop. Instead, I imagined their confusion as they stepped inside to find no one there at all, and no collected evidence either. It would take them a couple of minutes to work out what had happened, especially since my van was still parked out front.

And as if my luck wasn't quite bad enough, the scene guard at the rear of the shop was sitting in his police car playing shit on his phone. I expected him to look up and take some interest in us – after all this was his fucking job!

But no, he glanced up at us, and waved, went back to his game. I hope your fucking battery dies as you're getting a high score, I thought. Twat.

Shannon in front of me, and Nelson behind, laughed. And I admit I felt like joining them; it was laughable, and the ease with which we all ambled out of a crime scene was appalling.

"See, Eddie," Nelson gloated, "act casual and you can get away with anything."

I rocked my head side to side, mocking him. He laughed even more.

A dozen yards up the lane, illuminated every fifty yards or so by what Leeds City Council called streetlamps – and by what Yankee Candle might call one of their more subdued romantic products – we settled into a tension-filled silence as our feet trudged through puddles and mud, eyes growing accustomed to the startling lack of light.

"I think I'm surplus to your requirements now. How about you just cut me loose?"

I felt Nelson nudge me in the back with the gun. "Only way you get away from me, my son, is when I don't need you no more, alright?"

I swallowed. I didn't like the sound of that. There was no generosity in his voice, no charity. It was just cold. Business-like.

I could see over Shannon's shoulder the road running across the end of the lane maybe sixty yards away. I could see proper streetlighting, and I could see traffic. I swallowed again and knew this looked bad. There was a car parked hard over to the right so it wouldn't block any other vehicle wishing to pass. This was their getaway car, an old Audi four-wheel-drive; I just knew it. I also knew that if I got in that vehicle it was curtains. They wouldn't need me any longer and letting me live would spell disaster for them later. I'd seen enough action movies to know you don't let witnesses live.

"Zak, talk to me."

We were getting near to the vehicle, and I could hear the traffic running on the road up ahead, and I didn't hear any little tinny voice that you sometimes do leaking out of earpieces, any more.

"Zak? Where the fuck are you?"

My heart kicked a little. Something wasn't right here, and I felt the hairs on my neck shrivel away from the outside world – much as I wanted to do right now. I looked left and right but saw nothing but blackness. If I'd been thinking straight, I'd have dived into that blackness and hoped Nelson wouldn't shoot. But as things stood, my hopes and prayers had all failed miserably this evening – no reason to suspect things would change.

"Everything okay, Nelson?" Shannon asked.

"Shut up."

"What? I only asked—"

"Shut it!" Nelson grabbed me by the collar, pulled me back into the muzzle of his gun, and we proceeded slower, edging to the car. It was too quiet, too still.

From behind us, a car turned on its lights. It was the scene guard's car, headlights on full beam and seconds later an armed officer appeared from the darkness of a goods delivery slot to our left, and I wondered where the other one was. Nelson grabbed me tight and pulled me close to him – I could feel his breath, spitting quick in my right ear, the muzzle under his chin now, poking me in the right side of my neck. "Don't think I won't kill him," he growled. "You reckon you can drop me before I can drop him? Do you?"

Shannon froze and something like a squeal came out of her mouth, eyes those of a frightened cow, she now realised the consequences of making a shit decision. "I'm nothing to do with it," she said. "I'm on an attachment with CSI."

"Nelson," someone called.

Nelson spun us both around, and I thought it sounded like he was panicking – *I* would have been. But his voice, though loud, was under control, gleeful even. "Get the fuck back or I open up his head, okay? No negotiations, boys. You," he shouted to the armed officer, "put your fucking Tommy gun down and step back."

There was a significant pause.

"Shannon," he said, "go and open the driver's door, darlin'. Make sure there ain't no one inside. And you'll find the keys under the driver's seat. Start the motor for me."

"'She means nothing to me, she's just a fucking groupie wanting a thrill.' Is that all I was to you—"

"Do it!"

She screamed and then did exactly what Nelson had ordered.

His attention returned to the armed officer. "Drop it, cowboy." He laughed – and I don't mean he giggled, he laughed like a man who didn't know he was just a wrong move away from taking his final breath. And he found it funny. He found it hilarious. He calmed enough to say, "Do it now, there's a good lad, eh. No one wants to die tonight, but I hold the cards, okay?"

The officer put down his weapon and stepped back away from the edge of the lane.

"Nelson," that voice came again. "There's no need for any of this. Put down your gun and we can sort all this out without any bloodshed."

I recognised that Irish voice. It was DI Wilbourne. He sounded confident, he sounded calm, and he sounded in control, and I got the feeling Nelson wanted to be the one in control.

"Shannon?"

"It's clear," she said. "No one on board. Engine's running."

"We lifted the rest of your crew, Nelson. We got them both."

Nelson stiffened. "Fuck off."

Both of them? No, that sounded wrong to me. There had to be three more besides Nelson, at least. Two in the shop, one on the door, and a driver. I was tempted to offer that titbit to Wilbourne, but found it impossible to talk. Seriously, you can't trust your own body in times of crisis – I'd probably piss my pants next just to add insult.

"You're on your own. It's just you against the world. So put down the gun and step away from it. Do it now before things get any worse for you."

Nelson laughed again, and I admit it was making me nervous that he didn't care too much for Wilbourne's threats. It told me that he didn't intend drinking police station coffee any time soon. I don't blame him; it's shit. "Shannon, leave the driver's door open, and come and stand around here, darling."

She glared at him, making sure the coppers could see, and stood in the mud right in front of us, illuminated by the police car to our left and by a torch or a small lamp in front of us, probably where Wilbourne was standing. Apart from that, I really couldn't see too much. Shannon was standing a few yards in front of us, between us and Wilbourne when Nelson took his hand away from my collar and wrapped his left arm around my neck. Then he shot Shannon in the back.

The hot muzzle was back buried in the side of my neck again before I could scream.

Wow, I thought, it really was true love.

But I screamed. And I wasn't the only one screaming either. I could hear a female, possibly Jennifer, I heard Wilbourne gasp, but mostly, I heard Shannon screaming on the ground a few yards away.

"Try it, Eddie," Nelson whispered. "Really, go on, my son. If I gotta go out I might as well go with you. I ain't too fussed, know what I mean?"

Shannon's scream became whimpers and Wilbourne's confident voice had grown a built-in quiver; had dived from commanding to one full of supplication in one quick movement. "Nelson, Nelson. Okay, we're backing off. We're backing off, okay? Do you see us."

"Fucking thanks," I said.

"Can't trust no one, Eddie, eh?" Nelson laughed and dragged me up the side of the car. "Get in, slide over to the passenger seat." I did and knew this is where I would die. It wasn't even leather! He climbed in behind me, slammed the door, and kept the gun pointing directly at my head as he shuffled between the front seats and into the back. "Get into the driver's seat. Now."

I felt the gun in the side of my neck.

"Drive."

I didn't need to be told twice. I put on my seatbelt, selected a gear, and merged into traffic at the end of the lane.

"I really like you, Eddie."

I looked at him through the rear-view mirror. "Forgive me if I don't add you to my Christmas card list."

He smiled. "Just so as you know. I'll shoot you dead if you try to drive us into a wall or into the side of a truck. Okay? And don't go driving like a dick; I don't need the attention. We left your buddies behind and I don't intend picking up a tail, okay?"

"Why did you shoot her? You didn't need to shoot her. That's just being a prick."

"I didn't trust her. How can you trust someone who just changes sides like that? Seriously? At the drop of a hat, boom, she swaps from your team to my team, then she tries to swap back again. No way can you trust someone with no loyalty, Eddie. She was no good to me; she was a thrill-seeker, see? Tomorrow she'd have woke up asking herself why she threw away a career in the police for a life on the road with me. It wouldn't have lasted. Fickle. That's what she was.

"And I shot her so your lot would know I'm not dicking about, see? What is it they say? Action speaks louder than words. Well, my son, I fucking acted, didn't I?

"But most of all, I shot her for her own good. I done her a favour, mate."

"What?"

"Don't be a dummy, Eddie. Think about it. If she's careful and plays the game well, she'll say I had her hostage, just like I have you. She'll get medically retired or redeployed or whatever, and she'll keep her salary or pension or whatever. Bingo, she's a fucking hero and she's got it made."

I wrestled with his words but I didn't really have an argument to put to him. He wasn't stupid; he knew how people worked, and he'd read Shannon like a Ladybird Book. "Where are we going?"

"There's an old mill down Kirkstall way, not far from the Abbey. Someone's waiting for us."

Chapter Ten

The Gardener Revisited

AH. IT ALL MADE sense right there and then. "Zak."

I watched his eyes widen and I almost heard his jaw hit the floor, and I don't mind admitting that I felt a wee bit smug just then.

"Impressive."

"I take my hat off to you." And that little compliment wasn't there just to get on his good side – I didn't really believe this man had a good side. I believed once he'd used me to get away, he'd do to me what he did to Shannon. And though I'm fairly certain her wound wouldn't prove fatal, mine would.

He wouldn't let me see the light of day because I knew things about him now that no one else knew. And I could also point the finger at Shannon and ruin her credibility, dismantle her hero status. Why would he tell me about the 'favour' he'd done her if I could ruin it for her?

I sighed: trust me to get shot to death on day seven of a seven day set. Thanks.

"You wanted to streamline the gang, didn't you? But how could you do that without killing them? This isn't the Mafia, Nelson, is it? You have standards. These are your friends as well as the men you work with. Maybe you know their families, grew up with them. You couldn't just kill them.

"So you had them nicked. You kept all the dosh – because there's no point letting your men walk into a trap and lose it all, is there? You filled the bag with as much cash as you could. You pulled off your balaclava, and then you scared your accomplice into running. You told him your face was exposed to the CCTV, and you were staying behind to smash the hard-drive, eh?"

"Very good, Eddie. I like a man who can think while under pressure."

"Pressure? I'm not under pressure. I know you're going to top me. Nothing I can do about it." My hands were sticking to the steering wheel with sweat, my guts were doing triple summersaults and I wanted to be sick. One of life's natural-born heroes I am not. I am an average arsehole who would shy away from situations like this to go and read a book. But I didn't waste my time while he was making me drive loops all around the city to make sure we weren't being followed; I was always on the lookout for an opportunity. I wanted to do something, almost anything to get me out of this situation alive. And I hoped something would present itself. "Then you got trapped in the office. Was that on purpose?"

"No, no, that was genuine; couldn't find the back door key. But stuff like that has happened before, see. I was hoping to sit it out, and when you lot had cleared off, I could exit stage left."

I nodded. It figured. "Your mates walk out and get arrested. They know you're trapped inside. It looks to them like a job that just went wrong, doesn't it? There's no malice; they'd never suspect you betrayed them—"

"Turn left here, Eddie-boy."

"They'd never suspect you betrayed them. And when they find out that you never got arrested, they'll assume you were lucky and managed to escape. You and Zak teamed up again and everyone's happy."

"Correct. And?"

I nodded, the other plus point in his plan was a stroke of genius, really. "They'd never think of cutting a deal and splitting on you. They have loyalty."

"Man, I think I love you."

I drove along a wet road, streetlamps shining from the surface, and the stomach pains were getting worse as I could see the end of the road coming up quickly. I swallowed. I had run out of opportunities.

"Turn in here, on the right."

I did and we entered the darkness of a car park that was attached to a derelict old mill. One of those places with a thousand black windows and weeds that could swallow a man whole. "Where are we?"

"This is Cooper's Mill. This is your final resting place, Eddie."

I nodded.

"Park over there."

I turned the car in the direction he'd indicated, and I saw a vehicle already parked up, no lights on, faint glow of someone smoking a cigarette inside. The car we approached lit up as the door opened, and one man got out. I was maybe eighty yards from it when I put my foot down hard.

Nelson hadn't been holding onto anything. He'd been sitting on the edge of the bench seat, with his left knee on the central armrest just behind my left elbow. His right hand was in use – I know this because the gun was still in the back of my neck, poking through the two bars that hold up the headrest. When I accelerated hard, he was tipped back in his seat. There was no way he could remain sitting when I gave the car some welly. And the second reason Nelson was rolling around on the back seat was because his mind was focused on his reunion with Zak, and possibly on disposing of me too. He wasn't anticipating anything.

I used the only tool I had left available to me. The car. I'd strapped myself in, and as our car crumpled head on into Zak's, the airbags deployed and smashed the crap out of my face, more airbags deployed and protected my feet from becoming entangled in the pedals, and even a curtain airbag protected me from the side window as it shattered.

What did Nelson have to protect him?

Ah yes, a bag of cash and his super white plastic teeth, which, by the way, disintegrated when his head hit the dashboard at approximately sixty miles an hour. The gun ended up in the footwell, and his pelvis was crushed between the ceiling and the top of the passenger seat headrest.

I could smell coolant and hot oil, and steam roiled into the night, illuminated by flashing amber hazard lights. His shoulder was down by his abdomen. I think there might have been a slight collarbone issue there, I don't know. Prick. His face was a mass of blood as the shattered windscreen became a cheese grater. He was groaning though, like the low moan of a ghost, and he was trying to move despite his injuries.

I was bruised, my nose was on fire, my eyes wouldn't focus, my ears were buzzing, and I felt dizzy and nauseous. A soothing blackness enveloped me as someone approached, flicked a cigarette into the bushes and pulled out a gun. I blacked out as he reached in, unbuckled me, and dragged me out of the car, and all I can remember of him was inch-long grey hair growing out of his nostrils.

I'm almost sure he went back to the car, probably to pull Nelson out, I thought. But instead I could hear struggling, kicking maybe, and suddenly the groaning stopped. I might have been hallucinating here too, but I thought I heard an Irish voice mention something about loyalty to the crew.

Chapter Eleven

The End

I DIDN'T FAINT. LISTEN, I might have blacked out for a moment or two, but I didn't faint, okay?

Suit yourself.

I remember quite clearly seeing the lights go on. That shitty old car park was like a floodlit sports ground; it was lit up like daylight. I needed my shades! With that light came three armed officers at this side of the car, and I presume another three at the other side too, weapons extended. It was like watching some SAS movie.

But my attention left them, brought me to a black figure standing above me, weapon pointed at my head. I was really confused; they had armed police surrounding the car and not one of them seemed to give a fuck that a robber was pointing a weapon at me! I was confused and upset quite a bit.

It wasn't Zak after all. As the figure moved down towards me, the floodlights showed me Jennifer, with her arm extended. Jesus! "You okay, Eddie?" she asked.

"What?"

"You okay? You need an ambulance?"

"I need a fucking explanation is what I need. And coffee. And a cigarette. No, two cigarettes!"

She lit two, passed one to me and helped me to stand. "You were very brave, Eddie."

I was, wasn't I? I was very fucking brave. "Just doing my job," I said. "Where's Zak?"

"How do you know about Zak?"

"Nelson was trying to reach him."

She shrugged, holding onto me until I got my balance sorted out. I might have played on that a little bit, wobbled a bit more than I needed to just so I could keep my arm around her. "We got an anonymous phone call," she said. "A meeting place."

"Zak bailed out on him?"

"Looks that way. It sounded to us as though this Zak knew Nelson had stitched up two of the gang. So maybe Zak thought he'd be better off alone."

"Where's Wilbourne?"

"Had to take a call. He missed all the fun."

"Listen, be careful with that," I pointed to the smashed car. "It's got all my evidence in it, okay?"

"Don't worry about it. We'll sort it."

"Is he okay? Nelson?"

She shook her head, "Broke his neck in the impact."

"No, no," I said, "I heard him..."

"You heard him what?"

And then I remembered the Gardener. "I think I know why they've been so successful all these years."

"I think you're concussed."

"And what condition is Shannon in?"

Jennifer smiled a bit, "He shot her in the gluteus maximus."

"The arse?"

She smiled at me and tightened her grip around my waist because I was struggling so much.

Readers Club Download Offer

GET A **FREE** BEST-SELLER AND A **FREE** NOVELLA.

Building a relationship with my readers is one of the best things about writing. I occasionally send newsletters with details of new releases, special offers, and other news.

Sign up to the Reader's Club at www.andrewbarrett.co.uk and I'll send you these **free** goodies as a thank you:

The End of Lies is a first-person account of an extraordinary woman who takes on a Leeds gang boss. Read it if you dare. **NOT** for the faint-hearted or easily offended.

The Crew – a first person novella where you can climb inside CSI Eddie Collins's head and see the world from his perspective as he examines the scene of a Post Office robbery and finds something that makes him a target.

Acknowledgments

There's a long list of people to thank for helping to pull this book, and all of my books, into something that reads like it was written by someone who knew what they were doing. Among them is my amazing wife, Sarah, who makes sure I get the time to write in the first place.

To **Kath Middleton**, a huge thank you for making sure the first draft wasn't the final draft – you will always be the first person to read my books, and consequently always the first to point and laugh at my errors. It's because of you that this book has turned out so well, and it's because of me that you had so much work to do to get it there.

Thanks also to my Facebook friends in the UK Crime Book Club, my **Andrew Barrett Page**, and my **Book Group** for their constant encouragement – who knew readers could be so assertive, demanding… and kind.

A special thanks go out to my wonderful beta readers. This is the first novella we've worked on together, and I think our collaboration has been a huge success. Their time and effort shine through in the words of this novella, and I like to think they have made the difference between a good story and a great story. Thanks, guys – take a bow:

Shari
Fritzi Redgrave
Wayne Burnop
Alex Mellor
Janette Mattey
Gail Ferguson

Mike Bailey

Patti Holycross

And almost lastly (I've never been known for my brevity!), I'd like to doff my cap to a particularly wonderful crowd of ARC readers who've been kind enough to tell everyone out there about this book by giving their honest reviews of it. Sincerely, thank you, guys.

And lastly (go on, sigh why don't you), I'd like to extend my thanks to you if you're signed up to my newsletter (-**https://www.andrewbarrett.co.uk/welcome-home**) and offering your support, and if you made it this far, to you, kind reader, for investing in me, and hopefully for continuing to invest in me and my silly books – I hope between us, we gave you a little entertainment in exchange for your time.

Afterword

Did you enjoy this book? I hope you did. Honest reviews of my books help bring them to the attention of other readers. So if you've enjoyed *The Crew*, I would be very grateful if you could spend just five minutes leaving a short review.

I, and future readers, thank you!

About the Author

Andrew Barrett has enjoyed variety in his professional life, from engine-builder to farmer, from Oilfield Service Technician in Kuwait, to his current role of Senior CSI in Yorkshire. He's been a CSI since 1996, and has worked on all scene types from terrorism to murder, suicide to rape, drugs manufacture to bomb scenes. One way or another, Andrew's life revolves around crime.

In 1997 he finished his first crime thriller, *A Long Time Dead*, and it's still a readers' favourite today, some 200,000 copies later, topping the Amazon charts several times. Two more books featuring SOCO Roger Conniston completed the trilogy.

Today, Andrew is still producing high-quality, authentic crime thrillers with a forensic flavour that attract attention from readers worldwide. He's also attracted attention from the Yorkshire media, having been featured in the *Yorkshire Post*, and twice interviewed on BBC Radio Leeds.

He's best known for his lead character, CSI Eddie Collins, and the acerbic way in which he roots out criminals and administers justice. Eddie's series is six books and four novellas in length, and there's still more to come.

Andrew is a proud Yorkshireman and sets all of his novels there, using his home city of Leeds as another major, and complementary, character in each of the stories.

You can find out more about him and his writing at **www.andrewbarrett.co.uk**, where you can sign up for Andrew's Reader's Club, and claim your free starter library. He'd be delighted to hear your comments on Facebook (and so

would Eddie Collins) and Twitter. Email him and say hello at
andrew@andrewbarrett.co.uk

The Crew is dedicated to Violet Barrett, an incredible woman, and a wonderful mother, dearly missed.

Also by Andrew Barrett

Did you enjoy *The Crew*?
I hope you did. Why not try the other CSI Eddie Collins novellas and
short stories? Read them from behind the couch.

Did you know *The Third Rule* has been replaced by the new series
opener, *The Pain of Strangers*? It's already become a reader's
favourite. Have you read all the books in the CSI Eddie Collins series?

Have you tried the SOCO Roger Conniston trilogy?

CPSIA information can be obtained
at www.ICGtesting.com
Printed in the USA
BVHW071203100522
636623BV00017B/329

9 781739 659394